EYE TO EYE WITH DOGS

DOBERMAN PINSCHERS

Lynn M. Stone

Rourke
Publishing LLC
Vero Beach, Florida 32964

www.rourkepublishing.com

PHOTO CREDITS: All photos © Lynn M. Stone except p. 7 courtesy Susan Bahary Wilner, sculptor

Editor: Robert Stengard-Olliges

Cover and page design by Nicola Stratford

Library of Congress Cataloging-in-Publication Data

Stone, Lynn M.
  Doberman pinscher / Lynn M. Stone.
    p. cm. -- (Eye to eye with dogs)
  Includes index.
  ISBN 1-60044-240-4 (hardcover)
  ISBN 978-1-60044-320-6 (paperback)
  1. Doberman pinscher--Juvenile literature. I. Title. II. Series: Stone, Lynn M. Eye to eye with dogs.
  SF429.D6S76 2007
  636.73'6--dc22
                                    2006012256

Printed in the USA

CG/CG

Rourke Publishing

www.rourkepublishing.com – sales@rourkepublishing.com
Post Office Box 3328, Vero Beach, FL 32964

Table of Contents

The Doberman Pinscher   5

The Dog for You?   8

Doberman Pinschers
  of the Past   12

Looks   18

A Note about Dogs   22

Glossary   23

Index   24

Further Reading/Website   24

The handsome Doberman pinscher is a large, athletic dog.

The Doberman Pinscher

The large, highly athletic Doberman pinscher is both a companion and a working dog. Dobermans are alert, powerful, and fast. They love physical and mental exercise. They are skilled at tasks requiring both. Dobermans are used as guard dogs, guide dogs, therapy dogs, service dogs, and search-and-rescue dogs. They are also masters of **agility courses**.

DOBERMAN PINSCHER FACTS

Weight: 65 – 90 pounds
   (30 – 41 kg)
Height: 24 – 28 inches
   (61 – 72 cm)
Country of Origin:
   Germany
Life Span: 10 – 12 years

Dobermans have helped soldiers in war. A life-size, bronze monument of a Doberman stands at the American War Dog Cemetery in Guam. It is entitled "Always Faithful."

With its chew toy, a graceful Doberman bounds over an agility course bar.

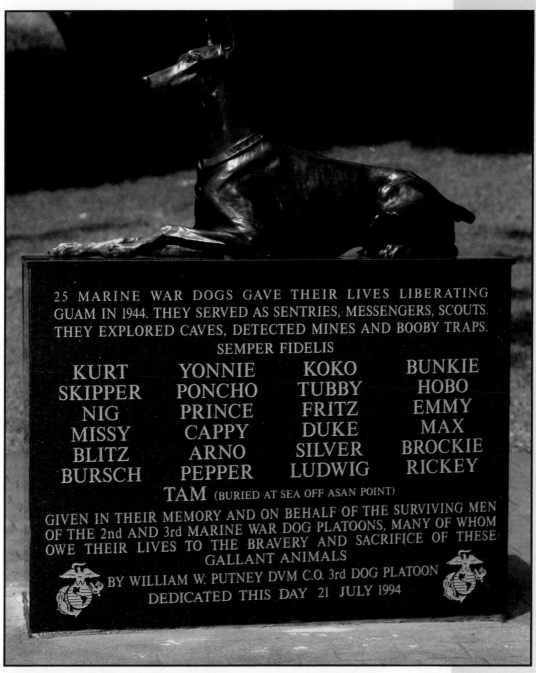

25 MARINE WAR DOGS GAVE THEIR LIVES LIBERATING GUAM IN 1944. THEY SERVED AS SENTRIES, MESSENGERS, SCOUTS. THEY EXPLORED CAVES, DETECTED MINES AND BOOBY TRAPS.
SEMPER FIDELIS

KURT	YONNIE	KOKO	BUNKIE
SKIPPER	PONCHO	TUBBY	HOBO
NIG	PRINCE	FRITZ	EMMY
MISSY	CAPPY	DUKE	MAX
BLITZ	ARNO	SILVER	BROCKIE
BURSCH	PEPPER	LUDWIG	RICKEY

TAM (BURIED AT SEA OFF ASAN POINT)

GIVEN IN THEIR MEMORY AND ON BEHALF OF THE SURVIVING MEN OF THE 2nd AND 3rd MARINE WAR DOG PLATOONS, MANY OF WHOM OWE THEIR LIVES TO THE BRAVERY AND SACRIFICE OF THESE GALLANT ANIMALS
BY WILLIAM W. PUTNEY DVM C.O. 3rd DOG PLATOON
DEDICATED THIS DAY 21 JULY 1994

A bronze statue of a Doberman, sculpted by Susan Bahary Wilner, stands at the American War Dog Cemetery in Guam.

7

The Dog for You?

Dobermans today are usually family pets rather than working dogs. They are loving companions, intelligent, and easily trained. Many owners enter Dobes in agility, obedience, and **conformation** events.

This Doberman is a pet and an obedient service dog.

For a Doberman, play time means snatching a Frisbee from mid-air.

A Doberman owner needs to have plenty of time for his or her dogs, including obedience training. Dobermans need plenty of outdoor exercise, but they are not well suited to be left outdoors.

Wise owners train their Dobermans to be highly obedient.

Early Dobermans were sometimes **aggressive**. Over the years, Doberman owners gradually developed more laid-back dogs. Dobes are still protective of their human families and, with training, can be aggressive guard dogs.

Doberman Pinschers of the Past

In the late 1800's, Louis Dobermann was a door-to-door tax collector in Thuringen, Germany. Dobermann's job did not make him a popular man on the street. He thought it would be wise to have a fast, streamlined guard dog. He just needed to find one.

Dobermans can be trained to protect property.

Dobermann began to develop a new **breed**. He most likely crossed a German shepherd dog with a German pinscher. Soon afterward, the black and tan Manchester terrier, greyhound, Rottweiler, and Weimaraner were probably added to the mix.

Louis Dobermann first developed the pinscher that bears his name.

The German shepherd dog is an ancestor of the Doberman.

By 1900, the type of dog that Dobermann developed bore his name and was a recognized breed. The first Doberman (English spelling) arrived in America in 1908. It became a popular police and guard dog in Europe and the United States. By 1977, it had become the second most popular breed in America. It is no longer number two, but it remains a favorite of dog owners.

Looks

The Doberman is a handsome, streamlined dog with short, shiny hair. It looks like the **canine** athlete that it is. A Doberman may be black, brown, gray-blue, or fawn-colored with rust-colored trim. It has long legs, a deep chest, and a long, straight **muzzle**.

The slender muzzle and sharp ears help identify the Doberman.

The first Dobermans in the United States arrived by ship in 1908.

In the United States, most Dobermans have **cropped**, upright ears and short, **docked** tails.

A pair of Dobie pups shows two of the common coat colors of the breed.

A Doberman sidesteps its way easily through agility course posts.

A Note About Dogs

Puppies are cute and cuddly, but only after serious thought should anybody buy one. Puppies, after all, grow up. Remember: a dog will require more than love and patience. It will need healthy food, exercise, grooming, medical care, and a warm, safe place to live.

A dog can be your best friend, but you need to be its best friend, too.

Choosing the right breed for you requires homework. For more information about buying and owning a dog, contact the American Kennel Club or the Canadian Kennel Club.

Glossary

aggressive (uh GRESS siv) – wanting to attack or attacking

agility course (uh JILL uh tee KORSS) – a series of activities requiring athletic ability

breed (BREED) – a particular kind of domestic animal within a larger, closely related group, such as the Doberman pinscher breed within the dog group

canine (KAY nine) – a dog or relating to the dog family, wild or domestic

conformation (kahn fer may shun) – the desired look and structure of a dog

cropped (KROPT) – to have been cut and set to get a certain look, such as the ears of some dogs

docked (DOKT) – to have had a section or all of a tail removed

muzzle (MUHZ uhl) – the nose and jaws of an animal; the snout

Index

agility   5, 8

American War
   Dog Cemetery   6

Dobermann, Louis   12,
   14, 17

exercise   5, 9, 22

guard   5, 11, 12, 17

Rottweiler   14

obedience   8, 9

Weimaraner   14

Further Reading

American Kennel Club. *The Complete Dog Book*.
   American Kennel Club, 2006.
Rayner, Matthew. *Dog*. Gareth Stevens Publishing, 2004.
Wilcox, Charlotte. *Doberman Pinscher*. Capstone, 1998.

Website to Visit

American Kennel Club Doberman Pinscher page –
   http://www.akc.org/breeds/doberman_pinscher/index.cfm
Canadian Kennel Club – http://www.ckc.ca/
Doberman Pinscher Club of America – http://www.dpca.org

About the Author

Lynn M. Stone is the author of more than 400 children's books. He is a talented natural history photographer as well. Lynn, a former teacher, travels worldwide to photograph wildlife in its natural habitat.